FIRE AND TEARS SERIES

Brightarrow Burning

Darkness Singed

Dawn Ignited

Fire and Tears: Series Collection Books 1-3

BRIGHTARROW BURNING

FIRE AND TEARS
BOOK ONE

ISABO KELLY

BRIGHTARROW BURNING

To my loving husband because he never asks questions when I pace around mumbling to myself about my fictional worlds.

And to my sons because they're finally giving me time to write.

CHAPTER ONE

I knew I'd find you here."

Layla Brightarrow flicked a glance over her shoulder, then returned her stare to the labyrinth of cobbled streets below. "What do you want, Ulric?"

"I'd like to know when you're going to stop trying to kill my brother."

"When he stops luring, capturing and selling my people." She felt Ulric move up close behind her but refused to flinch. Her every sense, however, focused on his presence, his movements, his breathing. Her muscles instinctively tensed, preparing for action, but she forced her body to relax.

"You know I don't condone what he's doing…" Ulric murmured.

"So you've said."

"But this is dangerous. For you."

She snorted, still refusing to face him. Ulric of Glengowyn was beautiful, sexy, and the man she'd been in love with since she was old enough to understand what those strange feelings in her gut meant whenever she looked at him. He was also an elf, and while he wasn't exactly an enemy now, he wasn't an ally either.

"Go away, Ulric."

"No."

"If you're so concerned about your brother—"

"I could care less about that traitor, and you know it."

She turned her head just enough to glance at him from the corner of her eye. "Do I?"

"Don't play games, Layla. You know I don't support the traitors."

She made a vague noise in the back of her throat to keep from giving him a direct reply and looked out over the cityscape again. From her perch atop the abandoned tannery, she could see several blocks into the Sorcerers' territory.

She tried to ignore the part of her heart whispering she could trust Ulric. The truth was, she couldn't be certain if he sided with Althir or not. They were brothers, after all. And when Althir, along with a number of other elves, broke Glengowyn's neutrality to side with the Sorcerers, he forced her to guard herself against Ulric's motives as well.

"Why are you here?" she asked on a sigh. "If you don't care if I kill him, leave me be."

Hard hands clamped onto her shoulders, and Layla found herself facing a very angry-looking Ulric. Her breath caught at the sight of him, as it always did. His dark hair silky and straight against his angular, pale face. She could just see the points of his ears poking out from his hair. His body was broad and well-muscled, bigger than the average elf, and so perfectly formed he'd been the fuel for her fantasies for years, even when she'd taken other men to her bed in an attempt to forget him. But in that moment, with the heat of his breath against her face, his eyes captured her completely. Dark blue and as sharp as lightning.

"How many times do I have to tell you this, Layla? I care if you get killed."

His hands tightened almost painfully for a moment, then loosened. For the sake of self-preservation, she took a step away from him. "I'll be fine."

"He almost killed you once already." Pushing the strands of her bangs aside, he fingered the jagged scar on her forehead.

She knew it was still an ugly red welt against her pale skin, adding to the many imperfections of her face, and she hated having him look at it. She jerked her chin to one side, dislodging his touch, then brushed her short hair forward again to cover the mark.

His jaw tightened and his voice deepened. "I don't want him to succeed next time."

"He won't. I know what to expect now."

"Do you?"

His mocking tone brought out her anger, which was so much better than her uncertainty and self-consciousness that she embraced it fully. "I learn from my mistakes, Ulric. I will kill Althir this time."

"But not tonight."

"Why?"

"Because he changed his plans."

She narrowed her gaze and studied him closely. "Why?"

"One of the Sorcerers summoned him and he couldn't refuse."

"How do you know?" But she'd already guessed. "You're still in touch with him. You still talk."

"He's my brother."

He glanced away, not meeting her gaze, and Layla's instincts leapt. She hadn't trusted him before, but now…

All the other elves had broken ties with the traitors, even if they were family members. Yet Ulric hadn't. He claimed he didn't care if she killed Althir, but he still spoke with him often enough to know his plans had changed? Why would he do that if he so disapproved of what his brother was doing? The only thing she could think was that he was helping Althir.

She clenched her teeth in an attempt to hold in the fury brought on by that possibility. Even if he wasn't directly helping his brother, Ulric was still in contact with one of the elves responsible for hundreds of human enslavements and deaths. That reality was betrayal enough.

"Leave, Ulric," she said, struggling with her disappointment. "Before I kill you, too."

He laughed, the sound so unexpected Layla actually jumped. She cursed herself for her idiotic behavior. Worse still was her body's reaction to his laugh. Her thighs clenched, her heartbeat sped, and her nipples tightened. Despite her distrust, despite everything, she wanted him so badly it hurt.

"You won't kill me," he murmured and closed the distance between them again.

"Don't be so sure. You've betrayed us—"

"I have not!" He gripped the back of her neck hard, bringing her face close to his. "Is that what you think? That I'm working with Althir against the Sinnale?"

"What am I supposed to think when you're still talking to him?"

"I do that for you."

She sucked in a breath. "That makes no sense."

"It does if you'd just believe that I don't want you to die. If I know what he's doing, where he's going, I can keep you safe."

"It's not your place to keep me safe. The elves chose their neutrality when the war began. You agreed with that position. You took your weapons and left us to our fate." Elven weaponry was their only defense against the Sorcerers. But after the invasion, Glengowyn broke off all trade with Sinnale, including those vital weapons. "Why would you care if I lived or died now?"

His voice dropped to a whisper. "I've always cared."

The grip on her neck softened, coaxed, drawing her closer so only a breath of space separated their bodies. Feeling the heat pumping from his skin, through his tunic and her heavier shirt and cloak, left her momentarily helpless. The air was damp, threatening rain, and she was cold after spending so much time on this rooftop waiting for Althir to appear. Ulric's heat drew her more surely than any fire. His fingers stroked lightly where her now short hair met her neck, and Layla shivered.

She didn't trust him and yet she found resisting him one of the hardest things she'd ever done. More difficult even than her first kill.

"I hate that you cut your hair," he said, his gaze traveling over her face. "You're still beautiful. But I adored your long hair."

"Long hair is a hindrance during war. And I know full well I'm not beautiful."

Just weeks after she'd nearly killed his brother, and almost died in the process, Ulric started to show up everywhere she went in Noman's Land, following her and trying without any subtlety at all to get her into bed. After years of treating her as no more than a friend, the daughter of merchants he regularly sold elf-weapons to, suddenly he was plying her with compliments, touching her, teasing her. As much as his continued communication with his brother, his attempts to seduce her roused her suspicions and heightened her distrust.

"You never believe me," he said, shaking his head. But his tone was teasing now, as if scolding a naughty child.

"Why do you keep the scar hidden?" he asked.

She glanced away. "It's ugly." It wasn't the only ugly thing about her. But it was the one thing she could cover. The gap between her two front teeth could only be hidden if she kept her mouth closed and she was too outspoken for that. Her nose was too sharp, her face too long, her eyes too far apart. Her skin was splotchy and her figure much too thin. Two years of war had taken their toll on a body and face never perfect enough to compete with the beauty of the elves anyway.

Now she had a scar to add to her imperfections. Yet another reason she didn't believe Ulric could really want her.

He brushed her hair aside again, catching her hand when she reached up to stop him. "It's a mark of your courage," he murmured. "You shouldn't be ashamed."

"Easy for you to say." How could he understand? He was a warrior without a single scar, not one imperfection, though she knew from her father that Ulric had fought in at least two wars during his long life. He was battle-hardened and yet still looked magnificently flawless.

"No. I hate that you have this."

He ran his finger over the rough skin and Layla

trembled in response. The slight contact sent heat radiating throughout her body. She started to lean into him, catching herself only at the last minute.

"It reminds me you were nearly killed. Every time I see it…" He paused and swallowed visibly. Layla raised her brows. He sounded and looked so sincere.

"But you shouldn't be ashamed of the mark." His voice dropped to a whisper. "And I need the reminder."

She frowned. "Why?"

He used the hand he still held to tug her a step closer. With only a couple of inches of air between them, his scent overwhelmed her. She'd always liked the way Ulric smelled. She used to make excuses to be near him when he came to negotiate with her parents and later her, just so she could revel in that scent. But now, there was a heady intensity that blocked the harsher smells of Noman's Land—the rubbish, the sewage, the ash of burnt fires and other things she tried not to think about, the hint of magic that was as impossible to describe as the scent of a baby's head but just as distinct, though much less pleasant.

With Ulric standing so near, with his eyes staring directly into hers and his hand gripping her, warm and strong, all those other things faded under the spicy, subtle aroma of him.

"You aren't answering my question," she managed to say, but her throat was tight.

"I've forgotten what you asked."

She was pretty sure that was a lie. He couldn't

possibly be as overwhelmed by her nearness as she was by his. But for the life of her, she couldn't see the lie in his expression.

She tried, gods help her, she tried to tug her hand free of his. She needed to step back, to put some distance between them. Instead, she leaned ever so slightly forward and her gaze dropped to his lips. A mouth she'd studied more often than she cared to admit.

"Please come away with me," he whispered.

The *please* almost had her. He'd never sounded so sincere, or vulnerable. Or quite so desperate.

But a very small and quiet part of her whispered, *He's still in touch with his brother. And you are trying to kill Althir.*

She eased back, using every ounce of strength she'd honed in the last two years. "I have a job to do tonight."

"Not tonight. Damn it, Layla, he's not going to be here."

She cocked her head to one side, studying him. Seduction had been replaced by anger—but there was still that edge of desperation. "Then I'll go looking for another elf."

She took another step away. When her back touched the parapet, she reached out and gripped the wood of her bow from where it rested always within easy reach. She held the weapon as a type of talisman against the draw she felt toward Ulric.

"Are you determined to get yourself killed?" he hissed. "Do you really want to die?"

"No. But I don't want my people to die either. The traitor elves are helping that happen. I intend to stop them."

He shook his head, his hair whipping around his face as his hands clenched into fists. "If I could kill them all myself, I would," he spit out. "This is too much."

"But you can't kill them. Any more than any other elf can. That's why I'm here."

"I know my king and queen have come to an arrangement with the human council. Your fresh quiver of elf arrows is more than enough proof."

She already knew he'd guessed his government was now working with hers, despite their initial call of neutrality. But they'd never discussed the situation. She had no idea how he felt about the deal.

"Do you disapprove?" Now that they were talking about the previously unspoken subject, she couldn't stop from asking, though she warned herself he might well lie. He was here trying to seduce her to keep her from killing his brother.

"I approve," he said without hesitation. "I never thought we should remain neutral. What's to stop the Sorcerers from turning their attention to Glengowyn once Sinnale falls?"

"Your weapons. Your magic."

He scowled at her matter-of-fact tone. "Only for so

long. With the strength gained by conquering Sinnale, the Sorcerers would be formidable enemies."

"Then why did your people choose neutrality?"

"They believed in the strength of their magic and weaponry."

She turned away to look out over the battered buildings surrounding them. "And the defection of some of their own people changed this belief?"

"It brought us into the war."

"Yet the king and queen are keeping their cooperation with our council secret."

"There are still those in Glengowyn who want to remain neutral—most of the elves wish to remain that way. They've…disowned the traitors. It's a handy way of disavowing any part in their duplicity."

She sucked in a deep breath as she listened. The air was sharp and humid in her mouth, tasting faintly of ash and mist. "So most of the elves would still leave us humans to die." He was silent for long enough she knew she'd hit a soft spot.

"I'm not one of them, Layla," he murmured. "I believe we should be involved."

"But on which side?"

His hands clamped down on her shoulders and she was whipped around so fast her feet twisted beneath her, costing her balance. He brought her up flush against his body before she could regain her footing.

"How can you ask me that? I'm betraying my own brother to protect you."

The feel of his hard muscles pressed against the length of her body made her stomach tighten. Blood pumped faster through her veins. Swallowing to rewet her throat, she opened her mouth to speak, closed it, swallowed again, then forced a few words out. "You expect me to trust you?"

"Yes," he hissed.

"Yet you still talk to Althir."

He brought his face closer, his breath brushing hot against her mouth. Her lips parted without her permission and need welled up to flow through her. His scent was impossible to ignore now. Something about it called to her, and she found it harder to resist the longer they stood this close.

"I talk to my brother to keep you safe."

"And that's the part that makes no sense," she said, her voice low and harsh from a lust she could barely control. "Why would you work so hard to protect *me*?"

"Because I care about you, damn it."

Her head spun as tension tightened in her gut. She blinked to force back the dizziness. "But only after I nearly killed Althir," she pointed out, as much a reminder to herself as to him. "Before that, you weren't here keeping me safe."

"I was forbidden by my king and queen."

She frowned, trying to see the lies around the haze of want fuzzing her brain.

His voice softened. "I tried to leave Glengowyn. To help you. King Varim forbade it. Until the other elves defected, I was stuck by their ruling."

His grip relaxed and he cupped her face in his palms. A shiver raced along her arms and up the back of her neck. *Step back*, she thought. *Get away while you can.* Instead, she dipped a breath closer. She barely felt in control of her body. So easy to just let go, to allow him to seduce her, to give in to what she'd wanted for more years than she could bear to think about.

"Layla." His voice dropped an octave. "They had to physically keep me away."

She shook her head and shifted her gaze from his, though his hands stayed in place. She couldn't bring herself to dislodge his hold. "No. That's…that's wrong. You never… Not before. I can't…" Why wasn't her brain working? Now she couldn't form a coherent sentence? She faced him again, intent on arguing, but as soon as her gaze met his, all the words evaporated.

Her pulse sped, and as she watched, his pupils dilated, nearly overtaking the blue of his eyes.

Suddenly she understood. Elf-fire. The pheromone that elves exuded whenever they were about to have sex, or at least wanted to very badly. The drug that drew humans to elves and was said to make the sex so amazing, humans often became addicted—which was why the pheromone was also nicknamed elf-tears.

Elf-fire couldn't be faked. It was a physical response, completely out of an elf's control. But they had to actually be attracted to their partner. While elves could have sex without attraction, though they rarely did, they could never pretend to have an elf-fire reaction.

Which meant, whatever else Ulric was after, he wasn't pretending to want her.

As she studied his eyes, watched the black widen more, the reality of the moment pierced her resistance. He was as affected by her as she was by him. She wasn't sure why. She just couldn't imagine what he saw in her to invoke lust. But in that moment, it didn't seem to matter. She'd dreamed about having him for so long. Even if it was just this one night. Even if she couldn't trust his other motives. She could trust his desire. And for a few hours at least, she could give in to her own.

"Elf-fire," she murmured aloud. She raised a hand to his cheek, then trailed her fingers along his neck, watching in satisfaction as he sucked in a breath. His hands tensed on her jaw, edging her closer. "Now do you believe me?"

"I believe you want me."

A low growl escaped as he stepped forward and wrapped his arms around her waist. "It's about damn time.

CHAPTER TWO

Ulric's mouth closed over hers. For a fraction of a second, his kiss was gentle, a silent plea for permission. But before she could suck in a breath or even accept the reality of Ulric's lips on hers, his kiss went from asking to demanding. His hold tightened around her waist, his head tilted to one side, and he kissed her with so much intense urgency, she was reminded of a dying man grasping for the one thing that might keep him alive.

Desperation overwhelmed any remaining sense of self-preservation. Her bow slipped from her fingers and both her hands found purchase on his solid frame. She couldn't have refused him then if the entire army of Sorcerers marched up to that rooftop. Pressing against his hard body only increased her insanity. Gripping at the muscles of his shoulders, the silky lengths of his hair, made her want more. Naked bodies, sweat and pounding flesh. There on the rooftop. Anything, everything he would give her. She wanted it all.

Only the barest remaining shred of sanity kept her from tearing his tunic from his body. "Somewhere else," she moaned against his neck as she tasted the salty tang of his skin. "A bed. I want you on a bed."

"The woods, Glengowyn…"

"No." She rubbed her breasts against his chest and sighed at the feel of his body tensing in reaction. "I have a place. Closer."

"Closer is good. Now would be better."

But closer was good. And closer was a place he couldn't know about, a place she'd never used before but had set up just in case. A safe house she'd never be able to use again after tonight. That didn't matter. The small, simple set of rooms would serve their purpose, giving her a secure haven to indulge for just this one night. And gods help her, she wanted to indulge, to taste and feel and suck and fuck until her body ached. And then she wanted to do more. One night. Just this one night. After, she'd be able to put this long obsession behind her and move on with her mission. Elves rarely slept with human partners more than twice anyway because of the side-effects of elf-fire. This was all she would ever get from him, so it had to be enough for her lifetime.

Nothing else mattered but quenching her need, answering the lust. And tomorrow she would walk away.

Because she'd have no choice.

Even that much reality was quickly overwhelmed by passion when his lips captured hers again. "Where?" he grunted before kissing her, making it impossible to answer.

When she could force her mouth from his long enough to speak, she said, "I'll lead." She tried to pull away, but he jerked her close again and kissed her. As her fingers tangled in his hair, she forgot what they'd been talking about or why she'd thought space between their bodies was necessary.

Then she felt him tug at her quiver strap. "No." She grabbed his hand to prevent him from disarming her here in the open. "Not here." Barely avoiding his next lunge, she snatched up her bow, then dropping it over her head to hang across her back, she spun toward the doorway and the stairs that would take them out of this building into the streets of Noman's Land. Her rooms were only a few blocks away, just outside the edge of Sinnale-held territory.

Tension vibrated from his hand up her arm as they made their way through the dark shadows, avoiding the infrequent pools of light cast by the few remaining working gas lamps. The Sinnale kept the lamps doused in and near Noman's Land. But Layla was comfortable in the dark. She'd traveled these streets frequently enough that even on a moonless night she could maneuver by feel alone through the twisting lanes and alleyways.

Darkness was her friend. And tonight it helped make the situation seem unreal, a dream in which she didn't have to worry about Ulric's true loyalties. In this dream, she could have him without fear or consequence.

The haze of lust filling her head didn't dim as they trotted toward their destination. In fact, it grew stronger with each step. She realized she felt drunk, out of control, loose and giddy all at once. *So this is what elf-fire does.* As the sensations continued to intensify, she thought, *No, this isn't quite like being drunk.* This was better, higher, brighter and more intoxicating than anything a man or elf-made liquor could conjure.

Unable to resist, she turned into Ulric and kissed him, her movement sending them both stumbling into a wall. He didn't stop her. He fell into the kiss, bracing one hand against the brick at her back to hold them both up while his other arm tightened around her waist. She'd barely found her footing again when he lifted her up onto her toes to better align their bodies. His hard cock poked at her lower abdomen, and she clenched in reaction as wetness seeped into the worn material of her undergarments.

"How much farther?" he hissed.

"Not…not far. Two blocks."

"Not close enough."

He ground his hips against hers and she nearly gave in. Against the wall of an abandoned building facing out onto the main street was fine by her. She didn't care if someone saw them. She wanted him inside her, fucking her hard and fast and now. Even the discomfort of her quiver and bow pressing tight into her back barely registered. All she could think about was Ulric.

He was the one who resisted this time. "A bed." He breathed through his teeth. "You deserve a bed."

She nodded, even if she couldn't quite make sense of what he was saying. Then she tugged him back onto the sidewalk, stumbling on weak legs for those last two blocks.

She pushed him into the alley, past piles of stinking garbage which she hardly noticed under the influence of the elf-fire. Or maybe it was just Ulric. When they reached the wooden side door into the building, she broke away from another kiss long enough to pull the key from a hidden pocket in the sleeve of her tunic and shakily insert it. The lock gave without a sound. They slipped into the dark stairwell, their hands reaching for each other again.

In the pitch blackness, Layla led Ulric up the stairs—she'd practiced here and knew the layout by feel. On the fourth floor, she eased open another soundless door, tugged him into a dimly lit hallway and managed to stagger to the fourth door on the left before diving into another kiss.

"Should get inside," she mumbled against his mouth, then immediately prevented his answer by licking her way past his lips to tangle her tongue with his. Only the sound of metal hinges creaking under pressure brought her up for air.

When she glanced behind her, she realized he'd been pushing at the door knob hard enough the wood frame was buckling. "Gods, you're strong," she whispered as a thrill of excitement tightened her stomach. She fumbled open the lock with the same key she'd used downstairs, then nearly fell inside as the solid wood which had been holding her up moved.

Ulric didn't wait for her to recover her footing. Instead, he followed her in, catching her up in his arms and slamming the door closed behind him with his foot. The reverberating bang made her cringe. It was late and the few people squatting in this building would be asleep. But any concern she might have felt was washed away as Ulric's lips covered hers again.

The darkness was lit only by light from the street filtering past a dirty window. They tripped and staggered through the small main room to the rudimentary bedroom. She finally allowed him to remove her quiver and bow, even smiled when he set them gently aside before roughly grabbing her up again. She had thought she'd feel more vulnerable without her weapons, that the spell of lust and need would weaken under her instinct for survival.

Instead, she felt freed. For the first time since the war started, she felt able to relax her guard and simply enjoy the exquisite sensations thrumming over her nerves. She didn't even worry that her survival instincts seemed to have shut down, because Ulric's hands were on her skin, under her tunic, and that made everything right.

Layla's breath caught when she landed on the soft mattress with Ulric's weight on top of her. The feeling was so perfect, so often imagined, that in the dark she could convince herself this was a dream. The strong, rich scent of his skin overpowered the musty, damp smell of the room. The feel of his hot, hard body against hers warmed her in the chilly air. Only then did she realize he'd removed her tunic as well as his own, leaving the thin material of her shift as the sole barrier between them. When had he done that?

"I should be nervous," she whispered as she trailed her fingers up his spine.

"Why?"

"I can't remember."

His grin flashed white in the dimness. "I've wanted this for a long time. But I'll stop if you tell me to."

Her snort of shock and disbelief echoed in the small room. "Right. That's going to happen." Wrapping her hands in his hair, she pulled his face to hers and kissed him again, allowing herself to fully fall into the sensation now that they were ensconced in the security of her safe house and the softness of a bed.

She couldn't taste him enough. Her hands raced over his bare back, testing his muscles, learning his body. She gripped his ass through the soft, pliant leather of his trousers and smiled when he groaned. His mouth moved to her neck, and she gasped. "Take these off." She tugged at his trousers. "I want to see you."

He left her long enough to remove his boots and trousers. When he rejoined her on the bed, her hand went right to his cock. She'd wanted him in her hands, in her mouth for so long she could barely believe this was real. He was hot and hard and pulsing in her palm. Without hesitation, she shoved him onto his back and leaned over his erection, letting her breath caress him. The muscles across his abdomen rippled and clenched. She met his gaze, smiled and licked the very tip of his cock. He hissed in a breath and his hips bucked upward. More than willing to oblige him, she took the full length of him into her mouth. Need and lust drove her to suck him hard and slow, savoring his salty taste.

His moans guided her, and she licked and sucked until she was sure he would come in her mouth. She wanted him too. She wasn't thinking of her own pleasure—she knew he wouldn't leave her wanting. But in that moment, with Ulric completely at her mercy, she wanted him to lose control. Cupping his balls in the palm of her hand, she fondled and squeezed, eliciting more of his groans. Her own body reacted to his pleasure. Wetness seeped down her thigh, reminding her that she still had her trousers on. Her shift was in the way as well, preventing her bare breasts from rubbing against his leg, but the tease of material against her nipples made up for the frustration. As she brought him closer and closer to the edge, she thought she might come too, purely from the pleasure of controlling his body this way.

"Stop," he muttered, reaching down to clench his hands in her hair.

She raised her head only enough to meet his gaze. "No. I want you to come now." And she returned to his cock, sliding her lips over him in a long, firm stroke. His head dropped back against the mattress. The tension in his hands remained but he didn't try to push her away. His hips bucked, flexing up to meet her downward movements. And then she felt his entire body stiffen. A moment later, her mouth was flooded with hot liquid. The sound of his cry echoed in the quiet room. She swallowed and continued to suck gently, drawing out the last of his release as his cock pulsed in her mouth. Finally, when his body relaxed, she gave him one last lick and crawled up the bed beside him.

"Did you enjoy that?" he growled, his voice breathless.

"Oh, very much. Did you?"

"Obviously. But that wasn't exactly the start I'd planned."

"What did you have in mind?"

He rolled her onto her back and stripped off her shift. His gaze fell to her breasts and she arched under the scrutiny.

"Shall I show you?" he said.

"Yes, please." The elf-fire raged through her system, heightening her senses. When his tongue touched only the very tip of her nipple, a sharp shock of pleasure raced through her.

"Oh," she gasped, amazed at the intensity. Then her breath left her as his lips closed over her nipple, sucking her hard into his mouth. Her insides clenched and quivered and she felt very close to coming from the movements of his mouth against one breast. Then his hands joined the effort, massaging and squeezing her other breast, pinching her other nipple until she gasped in near pain. She moaned and held his head closer, wanting more of this treatment.

When his mouth left her breast she wanted to protest, but his lips were moving across her ribcage, down her waist, and that felt so good she nearly screamed. Everywhere he touched felt overly sensitized, her nerves ready to burst. Sounds she never imagined herself making filled the small room as his tongue dipped just beneath the waistband of her trousers to flick the skin between her hipbone and her pelvis. He stripped her boots and trousers off without his mouth leaving her skin. As he pulled her underwear down her legs, his tongue trailed over her inner thigh, and she clenched in reaction.

Then he flicked her clit with his tongue and her body arched up, tension unlike anything she'd ever experienced seizing her muscles, controlling her.

She jerked against his mouth. "Oh gods," she

groaned. "This is too much. Was this…was this how you felt?"

"Yes." His breath was hot against her damp curls.

"How could you stand it?"

"See for yourself." And his lips closed over her clit, sucking her hard.

She didn't hold out even a fraction of the time he had. She came instantly, crying out at the burst and pulse of a release that shook her to her core. The orgasm went on for a long time, longer than any other she'd had. Ulric refused to relinquish his hold, forcing even more sensation from her and she thought she might lose her mind as she screamed with her release.

When the tension finally eased, she was panting and trembling. Ulric released her and moved slightly away. In the cool room air, her nipples peaked and her body quivered, muscles jerking in after-effect. She only realized Ulric had been holding her hips down after he'd let them go. Every inch of her body felt both satiated and still wanting. It was the continuing need that surprised her. How could she possibly want more? How could she take any more?

She glanced down the bed to meet Ulric's stare. His eyes glistened in the dark room, still full of heat and desire. Before she finished catching her breath, he gripped her hips again and flipped her onto her stomach then pulled her up to her hands and knees.

"More," he ground out.

"But…" She'd never known a man who could get erect again this quickly after orgasm. Unless she'd taken longer to come than she realized, but she doubted that.

"Elf-fire," he said, answering her unspoken question. "And I need more of you. Now."

His fingers dipped between her ass cheeks and slipped down to her dripping entrance. She jerked, her body so tender she could barely take his touch.

"More," he said again, and replaced his fingers with his cock. In one hard stroke, he plunged into her.

Layla's back arched, forcing him deeper. She was beyond making any sound now, too overwhelmed by the feel of his thick cock stretching her walls. But the sound of skin slapping against skin filled the room. Each thrust of his hips pounding against her ass made her tighten and clench around him. His fingers bit into her hips and she savored the feeling. Sweat dripped down her cheeks. For the first time since she cut her hair, she was glad to be free of its tangling presence. It would only get in the way when she looked back over her shoulder to watch Ulric fuck her.

He met her gaze and pounded harder. The muscles in his jaw clenched. He was sweating as well, the moisture dripping down the smooth pale muscles of his chest. The sight of him only increased her pleasure. Reaching between her legs, she fingered her clit, adding just enough pressure to push her body the rest of the way to orgasm. In the storm of release, she found her voice again, crying out his name.

A moment later, she found herself on her back and Ulric was inside her again. His hips jerked against her as he pulled her legs up to circle his waist.

"More," he repeated.

With his heated word, another wave of sensation washed through her, firing her blood and making her pulse race. She realized this was the elf-fire at work but was beyond caring. She'd never experienced anything like this and knew she never would again. This was more than just elf-fire. This was Ulric.

She came again, and again. Until she could barely breathe and spots danced before her eyes. She'd never orgasmed like this, didn't even think it was possible. And still he demanded more.

"No, no. I can't. Not again. Please."

"Once more," he insisted. "Come. Now."

And she did, instantly, on his command. Her body was so far beyond her control, so full of pulsing reaction, she only knew he came again because his movements stopped. She looked up to see his face, tense and stiff, his eyes closed tight, his lips pulled back. She'd never found men attractive when they came. But the sight of Ulric's release filled her with awe. And what love she'd felt for him before seemed a pale thing to what she felt now.

He collapsed to the side of her and pulled her tight against him, wrapping her in his arms. She sighed, wondering how long she could remain in this blissful state. Elf-fire still coursed through her system, but the intensity had dimmed. Physical exhaustion slipped in, making her limbs heavy. With a sigh, she rested her head on Ulric's shoulder. There didn't seem to be anything to say. Words were a crude way to communicate after what they'd just shared, and so by some silent, mutual agreement, they remained quiet. His hand slid lazily up and down her arm, raising faint tingles in its wake. She concentrated on that feeling, wondering if her body would allow her to make love again tonight.

Before she had a chance to test her limits, though, her eyes drifted shut and sleep took her.

CHAPTER THREE

*L*ayla came awake suddenly and completely. Out of habit, she listened to her surroundings before showing any signs of being awake. Then she blinked her eyes open and stared up at the dark ceiling. She could feel the heat and weight of Ulric beside her and wanted to roll into him. But reality was setting in, and though daylight hadn't invaded their privacy yet, it was on the way.

She'd made more mistakes in one impetuous moment than she knew how to fix. Why, why had she given in? She could try to blame the elf-fire, and that was definitely a valid excuse, but when she got right down to it, she'd wanted a night like this for years. The fact that she still couldn't trust him only made the moment more bittersweet.

As quietly as she could, she rolled out of bed and

gathered up her clothes. When Ulric shifted, she froze, waiting. After he settled, she realized how accustomed she'd grown to holding perfectly still and waiting for a safe moment to move. She hadn't always been this way. In her youth, she'd been full of impatient motion, never settling in one place for long. Ulric had actually started her on the path to controlling that restlessness when he'd taught her how to shoot a bow. Unfortunately, the war had done the rest.

She had to get out of here before he woke up, before the elf-fire caught her in its spell again and she completely forgot herself. She'd allowed him to lead her away from a possible target last night. His brother could still have shown. Ulric might have been lying about Althir's changed plans. She should have remained at her post and waited for her opportunity to kill the traitor she'd been sent to kill.

Pulling up her trousers, she clenched her jaw to hold in a disgusted snort. Instead of doing her job, she'd dragged Ulric to one of her few safe houses inside the relatively deserted section of city between the Sinnale border and the Sorcerers' border. This room was useless to her now, and with the coming day, she regretted that loss. Finding safe places to hide inside Noman's Land was difficult. Both her people and the Sorcerers' minions roamed these streets, each looking for weaknesses in the other's defenses. She'd sacrificed this rare haven for one night of sex.

Worse, she felt as if she'd betrayed her people merely by being with an elf. She had no idea of Ulric's true loyalties. Though she desperately wanted to believe all he'd told her last night. She was so giddy in love with him that if no other lives were at stake, she would hand herself into his keeping, the results be damned. A terrifying truth.

She stuffed her feet into her boots and dropped her quiver and bow over her head, adjusting the quiver strap across her chest. Glancing back toward the bedroom, she swallowed hard. She loved him. Damn it all to the sacred hells, she loved him. She wanted him again, even now. And yet, she knew better.

Or did she? Could she trust him? He'd been trying to convince her for weeks that she could. And the elf-fire was real. He couldn't fake that.

But she couldn't afford to trust him, even if she wanted to. He was still in contact with his brother. There was just no way to be sure he wouldn't hand her and her city over to Althir and the Sorcerers. At least no way she dared risk with so many lives at stake.

Which meant she could never see Ulric again.

She left the safety of the building and slid into the predawn air, keeping close to the shadows out of habit. Turning at every sound, scanning the streets for any signs of minion patrols, she made her way to the nearest Sinnale guard post. From there, she'd go on to the council and hope her mother and father didn't realize she was lying when she explained why she didn't complete her mission. They'd always been honest with each other—she was an only child and her parents doted on her. Keeping secrets from them was going to hurt. Though, she'd been keeping her feelings for Ulric a secret all her life so perhaps this wasn't so unusual.

Thinking about him again made her chest ache, both guilt and longing twisting her emotions into a ragged mess. She would have to avoid Noman's Land for a while. She couldn't risk seeing Ulric again so soon. Time had to pass before the effects of the elf-fire wore off. At the moment, she was even more vulnerable to him than she'd been before the elf-fire.

The sound of booted feet sent a jolt of adrenaline through her system. She melted against a nearby alley wall, tucking as far into the darkness as she could. As she scanned the street, she pulled her bow over her head, then slid an arrow from her quiver. The weapon would do her no good in a close fight. But she could use one well-placed shot to cause a little chaos and gain a few seconds' head start to run away.

The harsh stomp of a marching group neared. Minions. Her people moved more quietly. The Sorcerers' soldiers were too confident and cocky to hide their whereabouts. There weren't enough elven weapons left in Sinnale to harm them. Or so they thought.

She held her bow in one hand and silently nocked the arrow into place as a group of five minions came into view not two blocks away. They were heading back toward their own territory, swords in scabbards, gazes scanning the streets. Each had the sickly yellow hue to their skin that came from being in thrall to a Sorcerer. Even in the dim light of the approaching sunrise, she could see the dark circles around their sunken eyes and the glitter of red over their irises. They'd been human once, Sinnale citizens. Now they were enemies, so changed by the Sorcerers' magic, they were forever lost to humanity.

As they passed her hiding spot, one turned to gaze into the alley. He paused, falling a step behind the others. Layla remained motionless, her bow lowered but ready to be raised and fired in an instant. She held her breath even though she told herself to breathe. He was so close she could smell the faint scent of decay that clung to all minions.

After an agonizing moment, he moved on.

"You see something?" one said, his voice a wasted, harsh grunt.

"Probably just a rat," the minion who'd looked into her alley said.

"Check?"

"No," a third man, this one at the head of the group, said. "No time. The elves brought four more across the border last night. We're needed at the citadel."

They vanished down another street and Layla heard no more. But what she'd heard was enough. Sickness welled in her throat. Four more of her people, lured by elvish glamour and magic, taken by the traitor elves. And she'd spent the night fucking an elf.

When she was sure her way was clear, she hurried on to the relative safety of her border. Disgust swirled through her. Because even now, even with the guilt clogging her throat, if Ulric caught her, she'd go with him. Her only hope was to avoid him, to never see him again. The problem was, if he wanted to find her, he would. And she knew she was no longer strong enough to resist him.

CHAPTER FOUR

Layla managed to avoid Ulric for nearly a week. She stayed out of Noman's Land, using the excuse that she wanted to help her parents and the council improve border security. But she could avoid her real responsibilities for only so long. Inevitably, the council sent her back to the edge of the Sorcerers' territory, back to hunt the traitor elves.

At least she wasn't after Ulric's brother this time. That was something.

She stood on yet another rooftop, behind yet another parapet, in the blackness of Noman's Land, watching the well-lit streets of the captured section of the city. Her lip curled. The Sorcerers didn't bother to hide in the dark, the way her people had to. Their border was protected by sporadic and impossible-to-detect spells. Every time Sinnale spies infiltrated their territory, they risked triggering one of those spells. And even if they didn't, getting caught in enemy territory meant a death sentence. Humans had no real ability to kill the Sorcerers either—not without the needed elven weapons which were so scarce now as to no longer be a threat. So of course they didn't bother skulking around in the dark. They were winning the war.

At great expense to the spies who'd gained the information—four had been captured and were presumed dead—she knew that three of the traitor elves would be traveling close to Noman's Land escorted by a single Sorcerer. She was good with her bow. Even before the war, she'd practiced enough to become an expert archer so she could help her parents in their weapons negotiations with Ulric and the other elf traders. She could fire three arrows before the Sorcerer could find her. Killing all three elves was unlikely, but she would kill at least one. Maybe even two.

Chances were good she'd be injured too. Even killed. The Sorcerer *would* pinpoint her location before she could avoid his attack. But it would be worth it to take out at least one of the elves. And if she was killed…well, that was penance for giving in to Ulric and endangering her people.

She took a deep breath and calmed her nerves. She didn't want to die. But from the moment the Sorcerers had arrived, she knew it could happen any time. And if she was killed, she wanted it to be during the execution of a worthy mission for her people.

She stared at the brightly lit street, keeping well to the shadows. She had her bow in hand but hadn't pulled an arrow yet. The time was drawing near.

Even as her body took on the stillness of a statue, she heard the sound of the approaching carriage. It rolled around a corner, clattering against the cobblestones, the horses' hooves clicking loudly in the still night air. The window shades were pulled tight. The Sorcerer and the three elves were inside. She was certain of that, even if she couldn't see them.

She raised a small palm-sized mirror and signaled the team ahead of the carriage, the group that would cause a distraction so she could attempt the assassinations.

The Sorcerer would know what they were trying to do, but he wouldn't be able to find her until it was too late. Thanks to the elf king and the charm that hung around her neck, she would remain hidden to magical senses until she released her first arrow.

A section of building ahead of the carriage exploded, throwing debris and rubble into its path. The horses squealed in protest and reared back. The coachman had them back under control quickly—he was a human slave, she noticed —but their path was blocked, and the narrow road didn't allow them to turn the carriage easily to take another route.

As anticipated, the Sorcerer immediately stepped

from the carriage and signaled those inside to remain. He closed the door, but the moment's exposure was enough. She knew the elves' positions inside the carriage. Her arrows would slice easily through the shades, slowing fractionally, but not enough to keep from being deadly.

She watched the Sorcerer scan the rooftops. She remained in shadow as she pulled out her first arrow. Those years of practice ensured she could fire each quickly and accurately. She steadied the first against her bow and drew the string back.

The Sorcerer would have put a protective spell on the carriage, but it was no good against elf arrows.

She sighted, aiming for the point at which she was certain one of the traitor elves sat, and fired. She pulled the next arrow, nocked it and fired again, then a third time, so quickly the first arrow had only just sliced through the shade when the final arrow left her bow.

An instant later, the parapet not four feet from her exploded in a molten blast of magic flame.

She dove for cover, away from the first shot, but obviously the Sorcerer had anticipated that because the wall two feet in front of her also exploded.

Crawling as quickly as she could, she made her way to the opposite side of the rooftop. The building shook beneath her, forcing her to her stomach. She glanced back and realized the area where she'd stood had turned into a blazing, melting tumult.

And the building was going to collapse out from under her before she could reach safety.

With a renewed sense of desperation, she scrambled toward the still solid end of the roof. If she could just make the next building, she could escape.

The sides of the building started to melt, blocking the easiest exits. Amidst the stench of sulfur and the air-stealing heat, she scrambled to the only safe edge. But that side of the building was farther away from its closest neighbor. Escape was a long jump and she'd have to get a running start to make it.

Unfortunately, she was quickly losing room to make that needed run.

She stood, despite the fact that it exposed her to the still-falling rain of magic fire, and started to sprint. The wood floor beneath her was quickly melting away. She slipped, slamming onto her hands and knees, as the building shuddered again.

Too late, she thought, even as she scrambled back to her feet and dove for the edge of the roof. She couldn't make the leap now. It was too far. She looked down frantically for a railing she might drop to, but this side of the building was smooth brick, not even a window ledge to aim for. Behind her, the fire roared, sucking oxygen from her lungs and coating her in sweat.

She cried out in frustration and fear. A slow death by fire was too horrific to contemplate. There was no smoke to choke her first, to send her into unconsciousness before the fire caught her. No, the Sorcerer made sure she would burn, horribly and fully conscious. Her only consolation was the building would probably collapse quickly and she would die in the fall.

She looked at the rapidly approaching lava-like roll of fire and heat. She could jump, take her death into her own hands. Would slamming into the cobbles below be easier than flame? Probably not. But it might be quicker.

Still, she hesitated. It wasn't in her nature to commit suicide, despite the job she did for the war effort.

Her brain and body balked at taking that last leap.

She watched the melting roof drip away, watched the last few yards of safety evaporate.

And then she heard something over the roar of magic flames, the sound of her name. She looked to the neighboring rooftop, thinking it was one of the other team members. The sight of Ulric, magnificent in his rage as he signaled to her, took her breath away. She looked down and realized he'd pushed a plank across the gap between buildings.

She didn't hesitate. The flames were too close. She crawled onto the thick wood and scrambled toward safety. When the building behind her shook, her precarious hold teetered. She clung to the wood, her eyes closed for an instant. Then she pushed back to her knees and crawled as fast as she could.

Ulric swept her off the plank and into his arms just as the other end started to burn. He pushed away the part he'd been bracing, letting it topple in a fiery line to the cobbles. Then he wrapped her close and gave her a quick, fierce hug. She barely had time to register the hug before he was pulling her across the rooftop to yet another building. This time, the jump was easy, only a foot of space to leap. From there, he led her down an external stairway and into the dark streets. Her night vision shot from the fire, Layla clenched Ulric's hand and fought to keep her feet under her as she ran blindly behind him through the alleyways.

When they finally stopped, she could barely draw a breath. She bent over and worked to get oxygen into her straining lungs. She could still taste the sulfur in the back of her mouth.

When her breathing finally started to return to normal, the reality of being alive sank in. She glanced up to see Ulric standing over her, breathing normally, his face a stone mask of anger as he glared.

She met his gaze, then threw herself into his arms, hugging him tight. She was sure it was the adrenaline, the near-death experience, but she wanted nothing in that moment so much as to hold him. She wasn't even sure how to thank him for her rescue. She'd have to figure that out later. Now, she needed the solid reality of his body against hers, a confirmation of her survival.

His arms locked around her, keeping her close. And then his mouth found hers. She didn't resist, didn't question. All her self-talk about never seeing him again, never allowing him to seduce her, went out the window in that minute. It didn't matter if he was working with his brother or not. He'd just saved her life. After a week of her avoiding him, he'd still found her and helped her. And she'd never wanted a man more in her life.

Their kiss was fierce and hungry. His lips hard against hers, almost bruising, fired her need. She devoured him, soaked him up, melted into him. And it still wasn't enough.

She felt the rise of the elf-fire, felt it intensify a desire that was already overwhelming. She ripped her mouth from his and cried out at the sensation. Her alert nerves screamed. A part of her wanted to push away. This was too much, too strong. She needed to calm down a little first so she could handle the power of the pheromone's effect.

But Ulric wouldn't let her. He ran his lips over her throat, more gently, but the feel was a line of ice and fire, making her insides shake.

"Please," she panted out, "I…I can't…it's too much."

But he didn't stop. His hand cupped her breast through her tunic, kneading her firmly. His touch was solid and gentle at the same time, as if he was trying to control the excess of sensation.

"I have to…" he muttered against her neck. "I can't let you go."

She moaned, unable to stop herself. His words were more delectable than any of the physical feelings. Her reaction seemed to intensify his hunger, though, because his gentle touch turned rough again, desperation in his groan.

"Layla." His mouth descended on hers.

Her body shook against the need. Too much. And not enough. The sense of being overwhelmed, the almost painful brush against her sensitive nerves, became welcome. Needed. She felt him everywhere. His hand moving along her spine made her arch. He squeezed her ass with his other hand and she rubbed against his erection, desperation riding her hard. She needed relief and she wasn't sure where to turn. To get away. To get closer.

Ulric took the debate out of her hands. He worked the lacings of her trousers loose and pushed the soft leather down her hips until they pooled around her ankles. Her feet were trapped, but that didn't stop him. He lifted her and she braced her thighs against his hips even as her feet stayed linked near his knees. She glanced down to see he'd already freed his erection from the confines of his own trousers and the sight of his straining cock made her overheated blood erupt.

Holding her around the waist with one hand, he moved her hips forward, positioning her so his tip nudged her opening. Liquid seeped down her thighs. The feel of him was a tease that only heightened her passion. She had a moment to be impressed by his strength—he held her entire weight without bracing against anything—then he pulled her hips down, ramming into her. And Layla screamed. He felt so good and thick and so damned right.

She let him take control of the rhythm because she could barely focus beyond the friction of his cock pumping into her and the bump of her swollen clit against him. Her orgasm rose quickly, painfully, and her body started to move of its own accord to reach that exquisite peak. With her shins braced against the tops of his knees, she had enough leverage to follow his movements and meet him stroke for pounding stroke.

He murmured her name against her neck, the warmth of his breath washing another wave of heat over her skin. And when his hands tightened on her waist and ass, her body finally broke. She came with another scream, a sound Ulric swallowed in a kiss. A moment later, she tasted his own groan as his every muscle stiffened. She clenched at his shoulders, holding him until she felt him relax again. Then she pulled back from their kiss to look him in the eyes.

What she saw there devastated her. Tenderness and fear all swirling together with a look of wonder. Did she look that way? She felt those same emotions. Could he see it in her eyes too? Did he know she loved him?

And was she just seeing what she wanted to see?

As she held his gaze, she knew she wasn't imagining the tenderness in his look.

"You came for me," she murmured, still amazed by that fact. "You saved me."

He didn't speak at first, just stared at her. Then he raised a hand to touch her cheek. He ran a finger along her face and up to the scar on her forehead, tracing the bump. "That's twice now you've nearly died.

I don't think my heart can take a third."

His words warmed her more than his body heat. "Thank you."

He touched her cheek again. Then loosened his hold so that her feet eased to the ground. "Come on, we need to get somewhere safe." He patted her bare butt once before letting her go. "We have some things to discuss."

CHAPTER FIVE

*L*ayla didn't want to talk. She didn't want the moment to end. But as she pulled her clothing back into place, she knew she owed him this conversation. If for no other reason than that he'd saved her life.

As he led the way through Noman's Land, though, a part of her started to doubt his motives again. He could have saved her life merely to earn her trust. Even after their last night together, he must know she still didn't trust him fully. Perhaps he'd come to her rescue to gain her confidence, to encourage her to give away valuable information.

She swallowed hard as he opened the front door to a relatively intact building. It had once been a travelers' hotel, with a popular commons for locals and travelers alike. She followed, despite her instinct to stick to places she knew were safe. If he wanted her dead, he wouldn't have saved her. He could still be turning her over to the Sorcerers. But at the moment, she was willing to take the risk.

She didn't want to believe Ulric would save her life only to hand her over to the enemy. She didn't want to have these suspicious thoughts. She wanted to trust him, to love him freely. But she couldn't stop the wary voice whispering in her mind that all Ulric's actions were part of a more nefarious plan.

The idea hurt now more than ever before. And if he did end up betraying her, she thought she probably deserved it.

He took her to a small room on the second floor, one of the guest rooms. There was a ceramic heater in one corner, a wash basin and pitcher in another, and a large bed filling most of the room.

He walked directly to the single window while she closed the door behind them. The lock was still in place so she flicked it closed. At least this way, if someone tried to enter through the door, she'd hear them coming. After studying the street below, Ulric pulled the thick curtains across the windows and turned to the ceramic heater.

He pulled out a flint and steel from behind the heater and she raised a brow. "Most of the basics have been looted. Anything that could be used for heat and starting fires was taken over a year ago."

Without comment, he opened the door in the side of

the heater and proceeded to light the pile of wood and tinder inside, monitoring it until a steady flame burned. Then he closed the door and faced her.

She narrowed her eyes and studied the room more closely. The bed was made, the sheets looked fresh, though it was hard to tell in the dark. As she stared at the mattress, a subtle light rose in the room. She glanced back at Ulric to see a small ball of white light floating above his left shoulder. An elf trick she'd always envied.

"You aren't worried about anyone seeing that light?" she asked as she walked to the washbasin. The pitcher was filled with clean water, and fresh towels were folded on the lower shelf of the basin stand.

"You planned this," she stated as she turned to face him. He still stood silently by the heater. Since he hadn't answered her question yet, she met his gaze and waited, refusing to speak until he explained.

"The curtains are thick enough to hide this small amount of light," he finally said. "And I've kept this room ready and safe for the past week. I wanted us to have somewhere comfortable to talk. I assumed after you left without explanation that your safe rooms wouldn't be an option."

"There aren't any chairs," she commented. "If all you wanted to do was talk, shouldn't there be something to sit on besides the bed?"

A smile broke through his serious expression, the first smile he'd given her all night. "I never said all I wanted to do was talk. But we do have some things to discuss first."

"First? You're assuming a lot."

"I think I have the right to those assumptions after what just happened."

"You saving my life or you fucking me in an alley?"

"Both. And the fucking was mutual. Now would you like something to drink?"

He gestured to a table by the bed and the bottle of wine. She nodded, wondering if he might actually drug her, then hating herself for the thought.

He poured two cups, took a drink from one, then handed that one to her with a mocking expression. The fact that he read her so well was humiliating. She took the ceramic cup begrudgingly and gulped the deep red wine. It was sweeter than she'd anticipated and went down very easily. Given the events of the night, her near death, the run through the streets and the passionate sex, she realized she was parched. She finished off the cup and held it out for a refill.

Ulric chuckled and poured. "Trying to get drunk?" he asked. "That won't save you from my questions."

"Just thirsty," she muttered before taking another slower sip.

"Of course. Understandable." He took a drink from the second cup, then motioned to the bed. "Make yourself comfortable. I'll stand." His smile turned self-mocking.

"And keep my distance so the *Shaerta*, the elf-fire, remains at bay for the time being."

"That would be good."

She climbed onto the bed and settled against the headboard, staying on the side farthest from the door, closest to the window. Just in case.

Then she waited. He was the one who wanted to talk. He was the one who would have to start. She'd as soon finish her wine and slink off somewhere to sleep. Inside, she snorted at her own lie. She didn't want to go anywhere. She wanted Ulric on the bed with her, she wanted to lose her mind again to the passion and the elf-fire. She didn't want to think about their situation or the war or anything else that reminded her a real world existed outside this room. She most certainly didn't want to keep thinking about the ways he might even now be betraying her.

Finally, he leaned against a wall and folded his arms over his chest, cradling his cup of wine in one hand. "Why did you leave without saying anything?"

He didn't have to clarify. She couldn't pretend not to know what he was talking about. She started to tell a convenient lie, then thought better of it. He would know and he wouldn't let her off with anything but the truth. "I didn't want to talk to you. I didn't know what to say."

"You regretted that night?"

"Of course."

His brows lowered and his eyes narrowed. "Why 'of course'?"

"I gave in to the elf-fire. It was chemistry, hormones. I wouldn't have done that otherwise."

"Because you don't want me? You can't tell me that."

"You know I want you. I've wanted you for years."

Now his eyebrows rose. "Years?"

"Don't pretend you didn't know."

He tilted his head and his arms relaxed. "I didn't, actually. You never seemed…affected by me."

She laughed, a harsh sound even to her own ears. "I was always *affected* by you. Maybe because you never saw me any other way, you didn't know the difference."

"But I saw you with others, other elves, other human men."

"If you didn't notice, it was because you didn't want to, then. I'm not that good at hiding my feelings. At least I wasn't."

He glanced at the heater and took a sip from his cup. "Maybe I didn't want to notice," he murmured, very quietly. He met her gaze and said louder this time, "Human/elf relationships don't… Well, they aren't common."

"Yes. Your people don't have a very high opinion of mine outside of trade."

"Is that what you think?"

"Isn't it true?"

He shrugged. "Maybe for some. But not all."

"Why then? Why do elves refuse to spend more than a few nights with a human before ending the connection? Because the elf-fire is addictive for humans?"

"That's one of the reasons. Probably the most common."

"And what are the others?"

He held his silence for long enough that she wasn't sure he'd answer. Finally, he pulled in a deep breath and held his arms out in surrender.

"Your lifespans," he said. "They're considerably shorter than ours."

That was true enough. But there was something else, something he wasn't saying. She opened her mouth to ask more, but he cut her off.

"That's not what I came here to discuss. We'll have time to talk about the implications of a human/elf relationship later."

She raised her brows in surprise, but he hurried on.

"What I really want to know is how you could leave without so much as a goodbye?"

"I told you, I was…embarrassed that I'd allowed the elf-fire to overcome my common sense."

"But you just admitted you've wanted me for years. Why resist?"

"Don't be obtuse, Ulric. We're on opposite sides of a war."

"I am not your enemy," he ground out. "I never have been." He pulled away from the wall and started to pace, dropping his nearly full cup onto the bedside table so abruptly some of the wine spilled out.

"I just saved your life and you still don't trust me? What do I have to do? Die for you?"

She turned her head, not wanting to see the hurt he tried to hide with anger. What right did he have to be hurt by her distrust? "You've just admitted you never knew I wanted you, or at the very least you ignored it. Then suddenly, after I nearly kill your brother, you start trying to seduce me. And you expect me to believe you didn't have an ulterior motive for that?"

"You know I want you. The elf-fire doesn't rise otherwise."

"The fact that you want me has nothing to do with the reasons you started trying to seduce me."

"I beg to differ," he said dryly. "I would not have attempted to seduce you if I didn't want you."

"And what made you suddenly decide I was worthy of your attention? When you'd shown no interest over the many years we've known one another? Lust and desire can arise after the fact. But that's not *why* you started to pursue me. Once the war began, I never even saw you until after I started hunting Althir."

"I've explained this to you. On more than one occasion."

"And yet I still doubt your motives. Why do you suppose that is?" She hated herself for what she was saying. She hated that she even remotely believed these suspicions. And she detested that, because of the war, she couldn't trust him. But then, if not for the war, would he ever have seen her as a lover?

"I knew from negotiating with you that you were stubborn. But I never realized how obstinate you could be." He stopped pacing and faced her. "You want the truth? I wanted to seduce you so I could convince you to give up trying to assassinate the traitor elves."

"Exactly. You were trying to save your brother."

"No," he hissed, closing the space between them and dropping his face close to hers. "I was trying to save you. To keep you from getting yourself killed. As you nearly did tonight! I don't want you playing assassin, period. If I had my way, I'd sweep you off to Glengowyn and keep you hidden away and safe until the war was over."

He snatched the cup from her hand and tossed it aside. The ceramic shattered against the stone wall near the window. Then his hands were on her face, holding her gaze. "I don't care if the traitor elves burn in sun-lava for eternity. I don't even give a damn about the war. All I care about, all I've ever cared about is you, Layla."

"But why now?"

"Not just now, damn it. Years. For years you've been there, in my life. And when you were nearly killed, I knew just how much it would hurt to no longer have you there."

His grip gentled, but he didn't release his hold on her cheeks. Shifting so he was sitting next to her on the bed, he drew her closer. "Layla, don't you understand? How can you be so clever and so daft all at the same time?"

"Daft?" She straightened, offended by the insult.

"I love you, Layla. I love you. How can you not realize that?"

Her bottom lip started to tremble. She bit down hard on the inside of her cheek to stop the emotional tell. "That's not funny, Ulric. And that's not very nice."

"I'm not trying to be funny or nice. And I'm not saying this as part of some convoluted plan to betray you. I love you."

Her whole body started to tremble then. And an actual tear leaked from the corner of her eye, rolling across her cheek. She shook her head. "Elves and humans don't have relationships. You just said the aging and the elf-fire addiction make relationships impossible."

"I didn't say impossible. Nothing is impossible. And what does that have to do with the fact that I love you?"

"You…you can't…"

"Why not?" He kissed her, a soft brush of lips, full of tenderness and question. "Layla, the *Shaerta* is only ever this intense when love is involved."

At his mention of the pheromone, she realized her skin was tingling and her nerves were sparking under its influence. "Really?"

"Without love, the effects are still impressive and addicting for humans. But nothing like what's happening between us." He pulled back to meet her gaze, a strange little smile hovering around his lips. "You've never experienced elf-fire with anyone else, have you?"

She shook her head. "I'm not attractive enough to draw the attention of an elf lover, even a temporary one."

"You're beautiful," he murmured. "Any man, elf or human, would be lucky to have you."

For some reason, in that moment, with his blue-eyed gaze steady on hers, she believed him. She believed everything he said.

"You love me." She heard the wonder in her voice even as another tear dripped over her cheek. "How is that possible?"

He chuckled. "I have no explanations. All I know is it's the truth. I never realized how much I needed you until I almost lost you. And then tonight… I would have gone mad if you'd been killed."

She touched the hand cupping her cheek. "Thank you again. I don't want to die, you know. Especially now." She brushed her lips against his. "But how can this work?"

"We'll figure that out later. Now, I just need you, Layla. Stay with me tonight, here. Don't sneak out in the morning. I want…I need to wake up with you beside me."

"Ulric," she sighed. "This is impossible."

"Do you believe me? Do you believe that I'm not trying to betray you now?"

She swallowed and tried to think past the rising heat

of the elf-fire. And she realized with some surprise that she did believe him. She fully and completely believed what he was telling her. He loved her.

The wonder of it must have shown in her expression because he smiled and pulled her close, finally allowing his passion freedom. His kiss was deep and hungry, his tongue eager against hers. She wrapped her arms around his neck and fell back against the mattress, taking him with her.

CHAPTER SIX

*H*is lips were soft as they glided over her cheek, across her jaw and down to her neck. With tiny nibbles on the tender skin, he brought shuddering sighs from her, and she clenched in reaction. The elf-fire was pumping through her, heightening her senses, making his every touch more intense. Yet with his slow, gentle movements, the effects of the pheromone were somehow different. The overwhelming need still rode her, but there was no longer the frantic element, the need to devour him instantly. Instead, every nerve screamed for the slow, deliciously thorough torment he was inflicting. She didn't want fast or frantic. She wanted, no she *needed*, this slow burning ache.

"Do you feel it?" she murmured as his mouth traveled to the edge of her collar.

He nudged aside the top of her tunic and ran his

tongue across her collarbone. The move made her gasp and dig her fingers into his hair.

"Yes," he murmured. "Still intense, but…"

"But…" She didn't have the words any more than he did. She only knew this time, the elf-fire was driving them to a different pace.

"I've heard of this. But never experienced it."

His whispered words heated her damp skin, raising chill bumps, and her muscles clenched again as wetness seeped between her legs. "What's different? Why…? Why is it affecting us like this? Because we made love earlier?"

"Because we're in love," he murmured.

She raised her head and met his gaze. "You know?"

"I do now."

"You were telling me the truth. You do love me."

"Yes. And you love me."

"I always have."

"I'm very glad to hear it."

She smiled. "Love really does make a difference?"

He nodded even as his fingers went to work unlacing her tunic. "Which is another of the reasons elves avoid relationships with humans."

"I don't understand. Why is this time different from the other times we've made love?" She shivered as he parted the material, exposing her breasts to the warm air. His gaze dropped and so did his mouth, taking one peaked nipple between his teeth. She gasped as the shock and pleasure of it tore through her.

He lifted his mouth to say, "Maybe because we've declared it? I don't know. I've never been in love before." His lips returned to her nipple, his tongue teasing the hardened tip.

"You've never been in love before?" The idea was enough to override almost all other thoughts.

"We'll talk about it later," he muttered around her skin, then sank against her, suckling hard even as he kneaded her other breast with his clever fingers.

She wanted to argue, but her body took over for her mind. They could talk about this later. Now, she wanted nothing more than to feel, to experience this new level of intensity and to wallow in his devoted attention to her pleasure.

Her skin hummed as his hands moved down to her stomach. The muscles contracted and her core tightened in anticipation. She could barely wait. Despite her earlier orgasm, she felt as if she might explode with just the faintest brush of his fingers.

He unfastened her trousers, more gently this time, and after removing her boots, slid the rough leather down her hips, over her thighs, trailing his fingers across her skin as he stripped her. Her muscles quivered. Her toes actually clenched, all for the anticipation of his touch which continued to sweep slowly and gently across her skin.

He moved up between her legs, gripped her thighs and settled his mouth over her. He flicked her clit ever so softly with the tip of his tongue. Layla arched up off the bed. She lost all track of time at that stage, washed in sensation, each tap of his tongue tightening her muscles. He increased the steady rasp of pressure with her rising tension, taking her toward a peak she could barely fathom. And just when she thought she'd explode, he eased his touch, letting her muscles unclench just a bit before once again driving her higher. Each tease only intensified her desperation, so that when he finally sucked hard and slipped one finger inside her, her orgasm hit with the force of a battering ram. Wave after wave pulsed through her, going on and on. Surpassing even the previous, intense, elf-fire-driven orgasms.

She came down as slowly as she'd reached her peak, blinking her eyes open when she realized they were closed. "Ulric…" she murmured.

He'd eased up her body and was staring into her face. He cupped her cheeks between his palms and slipped into her in one long, steady stroke. His thickness filled her perfectly. There was no other way she could describe it. He felt right, as if he'd been made for her.

Despite their previous encounters, this sensation was completely new. Before, he'd felt wonderful and she'd been relieved to finally have him inside her. Now… Something had changed, and everything was better, richer, more perfect. That shouldn't have been possible.

She'd thought each time he'd fucked her had been perfect.

"The elf-fire?" she asked when she saw his eyes widen.

He nodded, eased his hips back and stroked into her.

She arched and sighed. "Why didn't I know this was possible?"

"Because it isn't possible with anyone but me," he whispered in her ear as he slid into her again. "No one else will feel this good to you. No one else will ever be able to satisfy you the way I can. You're mine, Layla. You belong with me."

"Yes." She said the single word so quietly, she wasn't sure he heard her. But she kissed him to show what she couldn't say out loud. She was his. She'd belonged to him for years. And there never had been anyone else for her but him.

He made love to her with his cock as slowly as he had with his mouth, kissing her until she couldn't breathe. She came once, a fast, sudden peak that surprised her. But when the orgasm ended, rather than coming down she continued to tighten toward another. Panting, her hands clenching his shoulders, she pumped her hips against his harder, faster, reaching for more. His breathing sped as he matched her pace. And when she came again, he followed two strokes later, groaning against her neck as his cock pulsed inside her clenching passage.

They lay in each other's arms for a long while, Ulric

lazily stroking his hands across her skin. Each flutter of his fingers sent frissons of sensation through her already exhausted body, but his touch felt so comforting she didn't ask him to stop. She wondered if he was feeling the same sense of wonder and the almost painful over-sensitivity.

"I love you," he murmured into her hair.

He sounded sleepy and sated, his voice deeper than usual. She smiled into the darkness and hugged him close. "I love you too. We have a lot to talk about still."

"Yes. But later. No reality now."

"Yes." Relief sighed out on her next breath. She didn't want to abandon this euphoric contentment for reality either.

"Stay with me. Be here when I wake up."

Despite the exhaustion in his voice, his tone was pure command. A command she was inclined to obey.

"Yes," she murmured again. When she angled her head up to look into his face, his eyes were already closed. His hands stilled as his breathing deepened. She watched him sleep for several minutes, awed by the moment. She didn't want to sleep only to wake up and find this was all a dream. He loved her. He wanted a future with her. At least, she thought he did. They hadn't had a chance to discuss the future. But they would in the morning, she was sure. She didn't know how they would manage being together. The war made their situation difficult at best. But they'd find a way.

He loved her. As sleep finally dragged her under, she thought, with his love, she could do anything.

A knock on the door startled Layla awake. Sun leaked in past the curtains. She blinked and rubbed at her gritty eyes, for a moment disoriented and unsure where she'd spent the night.

Then the bed creaked beside her and she remembered. She rolled over to see Ulric climbing to his feet. "Who's that?" she asked, worry sending her from the bed to snatch up her clothes.

Ulric frowned as he pulled on his trousers. "Not sure."

"Who knows about this place?" She'd assumed this was a secure room. Gods, she'd slept as if safely ensconced in her apartment near the council in the Sinnale-held territory. Anyone could be at that door.

She pulled her tunic over her head and then snatched up her quiver, pulling the knife that was tucked into a side pocket of the leather case. Since she'd lost her bow running from the Sorcerer, the arrows and the knife were her only remaining weapons. In the confines of the apartment—and with no bow—the arrows were mostly useless. The knife wouldn't be much use against a Sorcerer either. But at least it was something.

Ulric glanced at her, still frowning. He noted the knife without comment, then crossed to the door.

Before he could open it, a fist hammered hard against the wood, shaking it in its frame.

Layla's heart started pounding. Whoever was out there wanted in pretty badly.

Over his shoulder and without looking at her, Ulric said, "Stay back." He motioned her toward the ceramic heater. It wasn't much cover, but it would be something.

She put the bulk of the heater between her and the door just as Ulric released the lock and let the door fall open. And suddenly, Layla couldn't breathe. Her heart raced, her brain screamed to run, her fingers clenched the knife, but she couldn't suck in enough air to make any noise, not even a gasp. In the dim hallway stood Ulric's brother, Althir.

He smirked as he strolled past Ulric into the room and met her gaze. "Hello, Layla."

CHAPTER SEVEN

ayla looked between Ulric and Althir, barely able to comprehend what she was seeing. Ulric looked annoyed but not surprised. Althir looked smug, self-satisfied.

Her heart plummeted in that moment. After all her suspicions, after all Ulric had done to earn her trust, after *last night*, she'd finally accepted that he wasn't going to turn her over to his brother. Only to come face to face with how wrong she'd been to trust him.

"I knew it," she hissed, holding the knife against her forearm, prepared to fight her way out of the room. "I knew I couldn't trust you!" She spit this last at Ulric, whose expression darkened further. Althir laughed which made her want to cry. But she didn't have time for tears. She had to get out of here.

"Where are the Sorcerers?" She spoke directly to Althir, no longer able to look at Ulric.

"The ones I brought with me?" Althir asked in that smug tone. "Why would I tell you that?"

"Althir." Ulric spoke for the first time. His voice was deep and dangerously quiet, the single word holding a note of warning.

Althir's smile dropped away and he looked almost sheepish.

"Why are you here?" Ulric asked. "How did you find me?"

"You think the Sinnale are the only ones with spies?" He nodded to Layla. "You tried to kill me. You. Of all people. We've known each other for years."

"You've been luring my people into slavery and death. You expect me to ignore that?"

"You're fucking my brother. What of his part?"

"My mistake."

"Don't," Ulric barked.

His tone was so sharp Layla jumped.

"Don't call this a mistake. Don't ever say that again."

"You're about to turn me over to your brother and you want me to be pleased about being betrayed? You still want me to love you?"

"I am not turning you over to my brother," he ground out. Then to Althir, "I'll ask again. What are you doing here?"

"I thought that'd be obvious." He chuckled and looked Layla over. "Does she share? You've had her what, two, three times now? Can't fuck her any more without consequences. I can take her off your hands if you like."

Layla didn't even see Ulric move. She blinked and he was standing behind his brother, a knife to his throat. She hadn't even realized Ulric had a knife. She gaped at the scene. Elves couldn't kill other elves. It was impossible. That was the reason the king and queen had come to the Sinnale to take care of the traitor elves. But still Ulric held the sharp blade against his brother's jugular as if he fully intended to use it.

"You will apologize to Layla now, brother. And then you will answer my question, and hers regarding the location of the Sorcerers."

"Why should I? You can't kill me."

A thin line of blood appeared on Althir's neck. Layla never saw Ulric inflict the cut. One moment Althir's throat was a pristine, flawless white, the next a well of blood opened and dripped slowly down. Althir's eyes widened in surprise, a shock he couldn't have faked. He reached up to touch the wound but Ulric warned him off with a grunt.

"What are you doing?" Althir demanded. "I'm your brother. Your own fucking blood."

"You gave up the right to my loyalty the day you turned traitor. Now, apologize to Layla, or I swear by all that is sacred, Althir, I will slit your throat open and watch you die."

"You can't. It's not possible."

"You know better than that."

Layla's gaze narrowed. "What do you mean?" she asked Ulric. "You can't kill him. Can you?"

"Of course I can. And I will if I have to."

"But… But… It's impossible."

"No. It's taboo. It's socially unthinkable. It's so much a part of our social order that even some elves have forgotten it's physically possible. But we *can* kill each other. Repugnant though it is for us." He leaned in close to his brother's ear and murmured, "But I would not find killing you so difficult, Althir. Remember that. For what you've done, and what you intended to do to Layla, I would kill you."

She felt her mouth gaping open and snapped it shut. Ulric looked and sounded as serious as he ever had. Before her stood the warrior elf, the soldier and leader he'd been at one time. And she understood now why her father had whispered the tales of his ferocious valor in battle. Deadly intent suffused his every muscle. If this was an act, it was an impressive one. Althir looked terrified, truly worried his brother would slit his throat. She could actually see his hands trembling even though she was the length of the room away.

She met Ulric's gaze then. "Would you really?"

"Absolutely. And I wouldn't regret it."

"For me?"

"Only you. I haven't been playing games with you, Layla. I didn't bring him here. And I have no intention of letting him hurt you or turn you over to the Sorcerers. I do love you. And I will kill to protect you."

Althir opened his mouth to speak but closed it when Ulric moved the knife slightly against his throat. He swallowed visibly and remained silent.

Layla straightened away from her place behind the heater and continued to stare at Ulric, trying to gauge his sincerity. Could this be yet another convoluted trick, a way to get her to the Sorcerers without a fight?

He held her gaze, looking serious and steady. He didn't flinch or turn away. He didn't blink. And she knew the truth. He would actually *kill* Althir. He would kill him to save her. He loved her.

Her shoulders relaxed and she let out a long, low breath. He raised a brow and she nodded. "Okay. Okay. I believe you."

The smile he flashed was full of relief too, and she realized a lot of his tension had been caused by her reaction, not his brother's presence.

"Shall I just kill him and get it over with?" he asked, sounding almost jolly now.

"Shouldn't we find out why he's here first? If the building is surrounded, it would be good to know by how many and where they are."

"Right. You've a point." He angled his head to look at the side of his brother's face. "Well?"

Althir swallowed again. "Are you going to move the knife?"

"No."

"There are no others. I'm here alone."

"Don't lie to me, Althir."

"I'm not. I'm not." He held his hands up toward Layla as if pleading for her intervention. "I swear on all that's sacred. I'm here alone."

"Why?"

His gaze flicked around the room, then settled on Layla again. "I need your help."

"Mine?" Ulric asked. "Or hers?"

"Both really, but hers specifically."

"You need *my* help? The woman who tried to kill you? The woman you were just threatening to turn over to the Sorcerers?"

"I didn't really… You just assumed…" He shrugged. "I said all that to piss off Ulric."

"That wasn't a very wise idea," she said, nodding to the knife still resting against his throat. "Why would you do that?"

"Maybe we should go back to the reason he's here?" Ulric said.

"I never thought he'd try to kill me," Althir muttered. "Just thought you were a toy to him. That's why I was taunting you. I wanted to humiliate him."

"Him? Why?" She studied both men as they fell silent. And her eyebrows rose. "All that was some kind of sibling rivalry? You want my help and yet you made me think he'd betrayed me because you don't like him?" Her voice rose on that last comment. "I don't believe this. I didn't think elves were supposed to engage in that kind of petty behavior toward each other." She almost laughed. "And here I was putting you all on a pedestal. Thinking you were all so flawless."

"You should have known better than that already," Ulric said. "If we were flawless, you wouldn't have been sent to kill the traitors."

"True. Which brings us back to why you're here," she said to Althir, though she was still a little bemused.

She'd seen Althir and Ulric together and had always thought they got along. She'd had more dealings with Ulric—he was the one who negotiated with her parents and her. Althir didn't have the same talent for bartering and didn't enjoy it like they did. He spent most of his time flirting with the local women and directing the weapons deliveries. She couldn't recall having ever seen the brothers fight, though. In hindsight, she realized she'd rarely even seen them speak to each other.

Obviously, there was no love lost between them. No wonder Ulric didn't particularly care if she killed his brother. But... "Why have you two been in touch all this time if you don't even like each other? If Ulric is willing to kill you, Althir, and Althir wanted to humiliate you,

Ulric, why were you two still communicating after Althir turned traitor?"

"Tell her," Ulric ordered when Althir didn't speak right away.

"After you nearly killed me, I got in contact with Ulric," Althir said reluctantly. "I wanted confirmation that the king and queen were behind the assassination attempt. I knew the Sinnale didn't have enough elven arrows left. It shouldn't have been possible for you to attack us."

"Is that why you turned traitor?"

Althir held his tongue until Ulric gave him a forceful nudge in the kidneys. "Power, all right?" he spit out. "We wanted power. The Sorcerers promised us... Well they promised a lot. Most of which they didn't deliver. But by the time we realized they were using us, it was too late. The king and queen had already gone to the Sinnale council. You already had the weapons and the leave to kill us."

"You're here to beg for your life," she realized.

"I'm here to make a trade." Althir raised his chin, as if offended by her wording. "I'm not afraid to die."

She wanted to disagree with that comment, but she held her tongue and let him finish.

"What scares me is the wrath of the king and queen."

She glanced at Ulric. "I don't understand. Isn't death the ultimate threat?"

Ulric let out a breath. Then he said, "You want proof

of my love and trust, what I am about to tell you is one of our most guarded secrets. Death isn't the end for an elf. We continue on in an afterlife."

"All cultures believe in some sort of afterlife."

"Yes, but an elf's afterlife is…proven. We know it exists. We know what happens when we finally, eventually die. We know what our next plane is."

"What is it?"

"That will take some time to explain. For now, just know we do experience another existence after this one. Unless, of course, the king and queen prevent our continuation."

"They can keep you from your afterlife?" She wasn't sure what was more shocking, that they had proof of an afterlife or that their passage into that afterlife could be prevented by their leaders.

"The royal couple is in possession of a…you would call it a curse. The *Or'roan*. If it's inflicted on an elf and he dies, he ceases to exist. Period. His essence is destroyed utterly. It is the worst possible punishment that can be inflicted on one of our kind. Even death is less feared."

"And my dear brother," Althir sneered, "favorite of the royal court, confirmed that the king and queen invoked the *Or'roan* on all the traitors before they made arrangements with the Sinnale to kill us."

"So if Ulric killed you now, you would stop existing? You would no longer *be*?"

"Exactly. There would be no future lives for me, nothing. I would be over. And I do not want that to happen. After last night, I knew I couldn't wait any longer to seek your help."

"Last night? Did I kill any of those elves?"

"I'm not sure how you did it, but you killed two and mortally wounded the third. He won't live for long." Althir cursed in elvish. "They promised us, the Sorcerers *promised us* that they would keep us safe from the assassins. If we continued to help them, they would protect us. Some help they proved to be. One man to guard three elves?"

"They didn't think we would prove as great a threat as we are," Layla said with no small amount of pride. "They underestimated our resolve and our commitment."

"Layla was nearly killed last night," Ulric murmured in Althir's ear. His knife moved ever so slightly against Althir's neck.

"Don't, Ulric. I want to hear what he has to say before we decide whether or not to kill him."

"Those elves you killed," Althir continued when Ulric eased the knife back, "they have ceased to exist. After their long, long lives, after all the lives they've lived before this one, they no longer are. I don't want to end like that. I don't want to end."

"How do you think I can help you?"

"Your parents are on the council."

She stepped forward. "The identity of the council members is supposed to be secret."

"What do you think we took to the Sorcerers as bargaining chips?" he said with some disgust. "The council came to Glengowyn to solicit our help. They were refused. But their identities were revealed to a select few. A few of those turned to the Sorcerers."

"Did you know about this?" she asked Ulric. Even she hadn't known the council had revealed their identities to the elf leaders before the traitor elves defected. She'd assumed the king and queen discovered who the council was only after they'd come to the Sinnale for help.

"I was one of the few who knew," Ulric confirmed. "Their identities were safe with me, however."

After all that had happened, and all he'd done, she believed him. She nodded and motioned for Althir to continue.

"I want you to persuade your parents to intercede on my behalf with the king and queen. I'll suffer any other fate—banishment, a clean death, anything they choose so long as they lift the curse."

"Why would I do that? Why would my parents? You've been responsible for the deaths and enslavement of hundreds of my people."

"I'll give you information in return. Information you could never get through conventional spies. The kind of information that could win this war for you."

That was a tempting offer indeed. "How do I know this information is so valuable?"

"The king and queen could always reinstate the *Or'roan* if his information proves useless." Ulric finally lowered his knife and stepped away from Althir. But he moved to stand between her and his brother when he did, still protecting her.

His gesture made her smile. "True. Can we trust this isn't a trick, some way of getting information back to the Sorcerers about our internal workings?"

"It could well be a trap of some kind. But if so, Althir will die under the *Or'roan*. We can make arrangements to prevent information from getting out."

"A spell? He could have a spell on him that we can't detect."

"I don't," Althir put in.

But Ulric stared at him, considering for a silent moment. "That's possible. It would take a lot of power, though. And I think the queen would still be able to sense such a spell. It's her unique talent."

"What about an assassination attempt, then? Could he be trying to get close to the council, only to trigger some spell that would kill everyone?"

"He'd get killed himself in such a case, and he'd still be cursed."

"None of that will happen," Althir insisted. "I'm here in good faith. I want to make this trade."

"You're a traitor," Ulric said. "We aren't going to take

your word. I'm still not convinced you don't have Sorcerers waiting for us."

"I swear, Ulric. I swear on the heads of the king and queen. I am sincere."

Even Layla understood that giving one's word that way meant something to an elf. But this was a man who'd turned his back on his people for power. And yet, if he was sincere, and if his information could bring an end to the war…

"I have an idea that should mitigate the dangers," she said.

Ulric turned enough to look at her while still keeping Althir in his line of sight.

"If he's telling the truth," she said, "it could mean an end to the war. We have to risk that."

After a long, silent moment, Ulric nodded. "What do you propose?"

"I'll need to leave. I need to make contact with my people."

Ulric stared hard at Althir. "Can she leave here safely?"

"Yes. I told you, I came alone."

"No one followed?"

"No. Believe me, Ulric, I do *not* want the Sorcerers knowing my plans. They would do much worse to me than the Sinnale."

"Know this, brother, if Layla leaves here and is

harmed in any way, I will make you wish the Sorcerers had found you first."

Althir licked his lips in a quick, nervous gesture. He believed Ulric's threat. She did too and it warmed her heart.

"I'll be back by midday. If the council wants to accept your offer, I'll tell you then and we'll make arrangements for your passage. But you will be examined first. You'll have to submit to that."

"I understand," he said, though he didn't look happy about the prospect.

She gathered up her quiver and dropped it over her head so it angled across her back. Then she pulled on her boots and took one last look around the room. When she was sure she had collected all her gear, she started to the door. Ulric stopped her at the threshold.

"Be safe," he murmured. "He may still be lying."

"I'll be careful. I've been doing that for a while now."

"I wish I could go with you."

She smiled. "I need you to keep an eye on him. I trust you to make sure he doesn't do anything to compromise my people."

"You do?"

She nodded.

"Good. It's about time."

He leaned in and kissed her, a slow, deep, passionate kiss that promised more when they had time.

"Can you two save that?" Althir said dryly. "I don't

want to watch if I can't take part. Unless, of course, you're willing to include me."

Ulric lifted his head, cupped her cheeks and said, "I will kill him slowly and painfully if anything happens to you. I may kill him even if nothing happens to you."

She chuckled. "Try not to until I get back with the council's decision." She gave him one last quick, hard kiss and left the room. Despite the danger and the possibility that Althir was involved in some kind of elaborate trap, she felt lighter and happier than she had in years.

CHAPTER EIGHT

Layla crossed the treeline border into Glengowyn. This was only the second time in her life she'd been to the elven city. Most of the negotiations for weapons with her parents had taken place in Sinnale.

She followed a rock-lined path, marveling at the rich greens and browns of the trees and soil, the smattering of colorful flowers along the edge of the path, the quiet call of birds and bugs, the scents of fresh earth, moisture and a faint perfume that was unique to the elven city.

Everything was so peaceful, clean and beautiful. Such a contrast to what had happened to her own home.

But now, for the first time since the start of the war, there was hope for Sinnale, hope that they could get back to the beautiful place she'd grown up in.

She turned down another path, following the

directions she'd received in a note carried to her by one of the elves' carrier owls. Outside of the council coming to Glengowyn to ask for help, no human had been allowed into the city since the invasion. This trip was a testament to her trust in Ulric. He promised in his note she would have safe passage. If he was wrong, she would be arrested by the elven guard any moment.

But the path remained clear. She soaked up the peace and quiet and tried to calm the tingles fluttering in her stomach. She hadn't seen Ulric since the day she'd brought a group of Sinnale soldiers to collect his brother. Althir's story proved true. There were no tracking or assassination spells on him. No Sorcerers or minions had waited for her to appear from Ulric's hideaway. And over the last two days the information Althir had been providing was proving extraordinarily beneficial. He gave them inside information on the vulnerabilities and resources of the enemy, and it was enough for them to arrange a counter-offensive. Up to this point, they'd been defending, retreating, giving way. Now they could push forward and attempt to take their city back. There was a renewed vigor among the Sinnale, hope for a future.

And the elves had agreed to start trading weapons again. Not just the weapons needed to assassinate the traitor elves, but enough to resupply the entire resistance.

They even offered a few special weapons they'd never allowed into human hands before—despite her mother's best bartering efforts. Magical weapons which would give them an advantage the Sorcerers couldn't predict. Even the traitor elves wouldn't expect the king and queen to hand over these particular tools.

The war would turn. It would end. And with luck, the Sinnale would come out on top to rebuild their city.

As she neared the location indicated in the note, her surroundings began to change. A small, blue stream trickled across the path. The green of the trees seemed to take on a slight glow. It was late in the day, approaching sunset. But the glow gave plenty of illumination within the forest.

As the external light continued to lower, the glow got brighter, the green turning a translucent blue, sparkling with pinpoints of white light. By the time she reached the white stone structure twined with the giant tree trunks, the only light was the blue glow and the dancing of white sparks within the glow. The structure was a rolling wave of smooth stone, interrupted by tall, narrow windows and walkways bracketed by golden marble columns. Stained glass covered every third window, while the rest of the panes were made of such flawlessly translucent glass, they were barely visible. A faint scent of honeysuckle painted the clearing in front of the house, the plants themselves climbed the low walls enclosing the clearing. She loved honeysuckle. It was her favorite smell next to Ulric's natural scent. Funny, she'd never noticed if Ulric smelled of honeysuckle. It would be amazing for him to avoid it given the strength of the scent around his home.

She stood just outside the low wall and took a deep breath. She'd never seen Ulric's home before. The sight was a little overwhelming. But more than the house, it was the thought of seeing the occupant that held her in place. She wanted nothing more than to see him. But a treacherous part of her was afraid he brought her all this way to tell her he'd made a mistake. He didn't really love her. He wasn't willing to enter into a relationship with a human who would die centuries before him.

The quiet forest music soothed her enough to get her moving again. She crossed the grassy clearing and walked up a short flight of white stone stairs to the dark wooden doors. Before she could raise her hand to the knocker shaped like an owl, the doors parted and swung open.

Ulric stood on the threshold, looking stunning in a deep purple tunic and black leggings. His hair was pulled back from his face, framing the strong, angular lines and highlighting his masculine perfection. Her breath caught. Would it always take her by surprise, just how gorgeous he was? And would she always feel inadequate and ugly by comparison?

He didn't move toward her and she didn't step inside. She couldn't seem to make her feet move. The silence stretched as they stared at each other. Nothing in his expression gave away his thoughts. And when he continued to stand still and not talk, she started to fidget, pulling down the edges of her cream tunic and picking at the soft cotton of her tan skirt. These were her best clothes, an outfit she hadn't dared wear since the beginning of the war, but her best was still a far cry from the splendor of his clothing.

Her movements seemed to snap him out of his silence. "You look beautiful," he murmured and finally closed the distance between them.

She touched a hand to her freshly washed hair and smiled at his compliment. "You look amazing."

He stopped very close but without touching her. "I like seeing you without your weapons."

"It feels a little odd after so long, but…not in a bad way."

"Do you remember me teaching you to use a bow?"

"Of course. My father bribed you." She chuckled.

"I volunteered. Though I made sure your father didn't realize I was volunteering."

"Why? It meant I was better able to tell when you were trying to sell us less-than-perfect weapons."

He shrugged. "It made the negotiations more interesting. You and your parents are some of the best I've ever bartered with. How could I resist making the process even more challenging? And I wanted to spend more time with you."

"You did? As far back as that?"

He nodded. "And despite the closeness forced on us during those lessons, you never once reacted to me. I was never sure what to think of that."

She snorted and shook her head. "I was a mess every time you got close. I'd just spent years learning how to deal with that response so I could function around you."

"You laughed a lot, though. I remember that well. I've missed that laughter." He fell silent, his gaze roaming over her face for a moment. Then, quietly, he said, "I'm glad you came."

"How could I resist your invitation?"

"After everything that happened… I wasn't sure you'd trust your safe passage."

"Ulric." She reached out and cupped his cheek. When she did, she felt all his muscles relax and his breath whooshed out audibly. "I told you, I trust you." She studied his face, watching his emotions play out in his eyes. "You were willing to kill your brother to protect me," she murmured. "How could I not trust you after that?"

He let out another deep breath and wrapped his arms around her waist. "I can't remember the last time I saw you in a skirt. You look very sexy."

She felt sexy under his warm gaze. "Your clearing is full of honeysuckle. I love that smell."

"I know. That's why I had it planted here."

"For me?"

"I hoped you'd come here someday."

His simple statement made her smile and the last of her own tension eased away. "I've missed you. I…I wasn't sure how long it would be before I could see you again."

"I've been in discussions with the court. Things are going to improve. Soon."

"Yes."

"I don't want you working as an assassin anymore," he blurted out, then looked annoyed by his own comment. "I had intended to work around to that, to be a little more subtle and charming when I posed the idea."

She chuckled. "That sounded more like an order." She leaned into him, settling her hands on his shoulders. "I'm the best archer in the city. In no small part, thanks to you."

"And you've nearly died twice just in the last few weeks. You've done your duty. Assassinated traitor elves, killed minions and even a Sorcerer early in the war. That's enough." His grip tightened and urgency colored his tone.

"I understand your worry, Ulric. I do. But you have to understand, I still have to contribute to the war effort. It's not over yet. The Sorcerers still pose a very significant threat."

"There must be something else you can do, some other way to serve your people and still stay safely behind the front line. I don't want to lose you after we've come this far."

Her heart started to pound hard against her ribs. "I

love you too," she said. "But as it happens, the council has already assigned me my next mission."

"Damn it, Layla, you can't—"

She put a finger over his lips to stop his tirade. "I'm to head the trade negotiations for Glengowyn weapons with the elf delegates. I'll be facilitating the exchange and movement of weapons into the city."

His mouth actually popped open. "Why…? You won't be on the front anymore?"

She shook her head. "The council has decided my experience in working with weapons and trading with the elves is more valuable than my skill with a bow. And since my parents aren't in a position to head up the trade, I'm responsible for the entire thing."

"That's a big job," he said quite seriously.

But she could see the smile edging his lips. "Don't look so smug. I didn't do this for you. I did it for my people."

"I don't care why. I only care that you'll be out of danger."

"Well, not completely. The Sorcerers may try to prevent or interrupt trade."

"I'll make sure they fail."

She raised a brow. "*We'll* make sure they fail."

"We?" He nodded. "I can live with 'we'."

He leaned down and brushed his lips across hers. But his comment brought up the other problem facing them.

His lifespan was going to be significantly longer than hers.

"At least we'll have a few years."

When he pulled back, she realized she'd spoken aloud. "I just mean, even if the war ends tomorrow, you're going to live so much longer than I will…" She trailed off as a funny look crossed his face. "What?"

"I have something to tell you, something that I will be trusting you to keep secret."

"What—?"

He pulled her farther inside. "First, let's get comfortable."

He took her hand and tugged her through his home, but she barely noticed the splendor around her.

She was too anxious about what he had to say.

He led her to a large, open room, the painted ceiling soaring high above where vines twined through slits in the roof to weave through the mural adding an extra dimension. Low couches covered with dark blue and purple cushions surrounded a fire burning in a large, open pit in the middle of the space. Thick rugs covered the stone floors, and columns and stained glass made up the walls. During the day, this room would be alight with color. Tonight, everything glowed in rosy overtones from the fire.

Ulric eased her down onto one of the couches, turning to face her while holding her hands in his.

"There's more to the *Shaerta* than humans know."

She was glad he got right to the point. She nodded for him to continue when he paused.

"Beyond the addictive nature for humans, and the… benefits to sex, there is an additional chemical reaction possible. It only happens between long-term lovers."

"But elves don't take long-term lovers among humans. At least, I mean, outside of us."

"And this is another of the reasons they don't."

"Am I going to die faster because of my exposure to elf-fire?"

"What? No. What made you assume that?"

"Well, why else avoid this effect by avoiding a human lover?"

"No, the effect is just the opposite."

She frowned.

"Your life will be extended. To match mine."

"What?"

"We'll have to make love a lot, to maintain the chemical changes."

She almost laughed. "That will be a difficult task."

His serious expression cracked a bit and a small smile slipped through. "After centuries together, you may not be so eager for all that sex."

"I'm willing to find out."

"You don't fully understand the implications, Layla. You'll outlive every human you know. We'll have to be together regularly, and that kind of closeness can test even the strongest loves. Very few human/elf relationships have lasted more than a single human lifetime before the lovers give up on each other."

"And what happens to the humans then?"

"They return to aging at their normal rate, but by that time everyone they've known is old or passed on. It's a difficult existence."

"So what are you saying? That we shouldn't try because we might not make it?"

"No!" His grip tightened on her hands as if he expected her to pull away. "No, not… I just want you to understand what you're getting into. I love you. I will love you for the rest of my life. I've lived long enough to know this. But you're so young. You need to understand. If we continue on, the elf-fire will cause this chemical change in you and it will be more than addicting. There are physical consequences to an abrupt stop."

"Like what?"

"The humans who've carried on long-term affairs with elves, when those affairs end, their bodies deteriorate and many of their minds have broken."

She straightened. "So if you leave me, I risk… insanity, physical illness?"

"I won't leave you. Ever. But if you decide to go… There's more."

More? She wasn't sure how much more she could take.

"The effects are actually worse on couples who aren't truly in love. Those who are in love, honest love, their lives together can be successful. Those are the couples we write songs about. They're legends. And they are rare. Most elves are frankly not willing to take the risk."

She stared at him for a long moment before speaking. "You're saying that if I don't really love you, if what I feel isn't…honest, then I stand to suffer for it later on."

"Yes."

She felt the tremble in his hands and watched his breath come more rapidly as she continued to stare at him. There was nothing in his expression to give away his thoughts, but she could feel his tension easily enough. She blinked as she realized he was worried about the strength of *her* feelings. He was willing to risk a long-term relationship with her, the kind of relationship most elves weren't willing to take a chance on. He believed his love was true and would last forever. He was worried hers wasn't. How little he knew.

She smiled. When he frowned, her smile turned to an outright grin. "Ulric." She leaned forward and kissed him. "I don't think we have anything to worry about."

"But…"

"Trust me," she said against his mouth. "People will write songs about our love. I promise. I've loved you my whole life. That's not about to change, even if I live as long as an elf."

He chuckled against her lips, then sealed his mouth to hers, kissing her deeply. She could already feel the elf-fire rising, washing over her, taking her into her new life.

"I love you, Ulric. Forever."

"Forever," he repeated. And eased her back into the couch. "But I think we need to make sure. We have a lot of lovemaking to do."

She laughed even as she arched up so he could pull her tunic off over her head. His lips closed on hers again, swallowing her chuckle. She wrapped herself around him and sighed, looking forward to the future more than she ever had before, a long, long future with the man she loved.

**Continue reading for an excerpt from the
next book in the
Fire and Tears series**

DARKNESS SINGED

DARKNESS SINGED

ISABO KELLY

DARKNESS SINGED

FIRE AND TEARS BOOK TWO

EXCERPT

CHAPTER 1

uala of Glengowyn kept her gaze forward and her shoulders proud but loose, determined to hide the tension twisting her stomach from the soldiers surrounding her. She hadn't been outside Glengowyn in nearly a century, most certainly hadn't been allowed to leave since the war between the Sorcerers and the humans of Sinnale began. This trip, necessary though it was, would not have been her choice for her first excursion back into Sinnale.

She rode near the center of the military escort—both human and elven—her bow and quiver bumping gently against her back, comforting in their familiarity. The less comfortable knives in the scabbards strapped to her waist were a steady reminder of the danger. Even the glowering, deadly elf riding beside her couldn't calm her anxiety.

But she'd be damned if she let Einar see her fear.

Lifting her chin to steady herself, she studied the grassy plains bracketing the road from Glengowyn to Sinnale. They'd left the safety of the forest not long ago, and she'd felt exposed and vulnerable ever since. The human city was in view, less than half a mile away, the buildings and houses rising and falling like a clunky, awkward mountain range against the deep blue sky. Beyond and to the west of the city, the real mountains of the Arei-atun Range rose up like purple and gray sentinels. The contrast between nature and the manmade structures was stark and sobering.

"You're hiding your tension well, my lady," the towering man beside her said quietly, for her ears only. "But your mare is beginning to react to your anxiety."

Nuala scowled at Einar then focused on her mount for several moments, working at relaxing her body, her grip on the reins, her knees against the horse's sides. She felt the large gray relax as well and only then realized how tightly the mare had been holding herself. If not for Einar's comment, the gray would have started fidgeting openly soon, revealing just how scared her rider was. The fact that Einar had noticed Nuala's unease so easily robbed any feelings of gratitude she might have had for his discreet help, though.

But she was nothing if not well trained to be polite. "Thank you. I will make an effort to control my reactions better."

"You have always been in full control of your reactions, my lady. To everything."

He didn't look at her as he spoke, his gaze sweeping their surroundings, ever watchful. But she heard the bite in the comment, the subtle jab most wouldn't have noticed. She refused to respond, not entirely sure she could censor herself in that moment. Not when she expected a physical attack with every breath. And most definitely not with *him*.

She kept her own gaze on the high grass beside the road so she wouldn't have to face Einar and risk him seeing her inner turmoil. He was the only man, the only person, who had ever been able to read her with any level of accuracy. Even her cousins, Ulric and Althir, who'd looked after her after her parents were killed in the first goblin war, could never read her moods or thoughts.

Einar was an entirely different story.

She acknowledged, reluctantly, that the danger posed by the Sorcerers and the war weren't the only reasons for her anxiety. When the Darkness of Glengowyn, personal bodyguard to the elf king and queen, had been assigned as her bodyguard, Nuala very nearly backed out.

But to do so would have revealed too much. To everyone. Including *him*.

"You will reach the city safely," Einar murmured. "I swear it."

She continued to stare at the grass so he wouldn't see her expression, though she was sure he wasn't looking at her as he spoke. His words made her throat squeeze tight. "I know you'll do what you can," she returned quietly. "But no caravan reaches Sinnale without being attacked. This will be no different."

"I'm not afraid of the Sorcerers' minions."

"Of course *you're* not." As soon as she spoke, she wished she could take it back. Too much. Those few words revealed too much. And Einar would know. He would understand everything if she wasn't very careful.

She thought maybe he understood too well already.

"You've no need to fear them either."

"I'm not the warrior here. I make the weapons. I don't go into battle with them."

"And I have no intention of risking you in battle now."

A traitorous part of her heart lifted at that. "When the minions attack, you'll have no choice."

He actually turned to look at her and because she could feel his stare on the side of her face, she met his gaze. Black as the deepest, moonless night.

"You think I will let those abominations near you? I have sworn to protect you as I would the king and queen. You doubt me?"

She realized he was actually offended. Most wouldn't have seen it. He hid his emotions better even than she did. Most of the elves of Glengowyn thought he didn't have any. But she'd always seen beyond his façade. The sword cut both ways between them.

"I don't doubt your ability to protect me, Einar. But if the traitors have told the Sorcerers about me, they'll be waiting for this particular caravan. You may not have the choice to keep me out of the fight."

"You're not trained for combat. Do not engage the enemy. Stay beside me, and I will see you safe."

She shook her head and looked away. He was the most deadly elf in all of Glengowyn. But he wasn't invincible. No matter what the others thought.

The one thing in her favor was that, outside of the traitor elves, no one from Sinnale had seen her in the last two human generations. None of the minions would recognize her—if they still retained any memories of their human lives after the Sorcerers were done with them. And she doubted any of the traitors would dirty their hands in an actual caravan attack. The Sorcerers never left the city, and none of them would know her on sight anyway.

The attack, *when* it came, would likely be no different from any other. The heavy guard surrounding her and the wagons of her arrows, both her normal enchanted arrows and the special weapons the Sinnale were only now being allowed to trade for, should have no trouble repelling the minions.

But as she studied the long, waving sheets of golden-green grass along the roadside, a chill skittered along her shoulders and her mare danced a step or two beneath her before she reined her in. Nuala's stomach tightened.

She hadn't been allowed to take risks of any kind since the end of the second goblin war, not since she'd developed the weapon she was now delivering to Sinnale, the weapon that had helped the elves win that war. Once the conflict was over, her particular magic, and her skill in wielding it, had been considered too valuable to endanger.

The sudden rake of terror along her spine could have had something to do with her lack of recent experience with tension and fear. Nothing in the grass signaled a change. The city's outlier buildings grew closer with each clomp of the horses' hooves, close enough now she could see some of the damage to the structures at the edge of Noman's Land, not far from where they would enter the city.

Still, she couldn't shake the sensation of being watched.

A quick glance at Einar, then the other warriors, assured her they were keeping their focus on the surroundings. No one paid her any particular attention. Not for lack of curiosity, she was sure, but because the Darkness of Glengowyn had ordered them to ignore her. Staring would not only distract them from the possible dangers, it would single her out as someone significant. The soldiers were following that order perfectly. She was outwardly no different from any other mounted elf in the caravan.

She studied the grass again, frowning in concentration as she searched the shifting waves.

That focus saved her life.

Don't Miss
DARKNESS SINGED
Fire and Tears
Book Two

BOOKS BY ISABO KELLY

Fire and Tears Series

Brightarrow Burning

Darkness Singed

Dawn Ignited

Fire and Tears: Series Collection Books 1-3

Fate's Hand Series

Thief's Desire

Destiny's Seduction

New York Empires Anthologies

Going All In

Icing The Puck

Roughing It

Kellyn's Sacrifice

The Last Guardian

Bonfire Night

ABOUT THE AUTHOR

Isabo Kelly is the award-winning author of numerous science fiction, fantasy, and paranormal romances. She also writes best-selling paranormal romance under the name Kat Simons. Her life has taken her from Las Vegas to Hawaii, where she got her BA in Zoology, back to Vegas where she looked after sharks, then on to Germany and Ireland where she got her Ph.D. in Animal Behavior. Now Isabo focuses on writing. She lives in New York with her beloved family and a library's worth of books.

For more on Isabo, be sure to visit her website or you can find her on social media. She loves hearing from readers!

For more on Isabo and her books

Website: https://www.isabokelly.com
Instagram: https://www.instagram.com/isabokelly/
Threads: https://www.threads.net/@isabokelly

KatSimonsBooks Store
https://www.tanddpublishingbookstore.com

KATSIMONSBOOKS

WELCOMES

 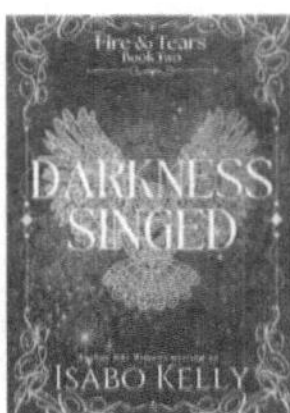  

ISABO KELLY

Look out for all of Isabo's books as they make their way to her alter ego's store where readers can buy direct from the author, get cool new merch, special editions, and more! Be sure to check out all Isabo's fiction at KatSimonsBooks

https://www.KatSimonsBooks.com

www.ingramcontent.com/pod-product-compliance
Lightning Source LLC
Chambersburg PA
CBHW030815200726
48288CB00004B/1249